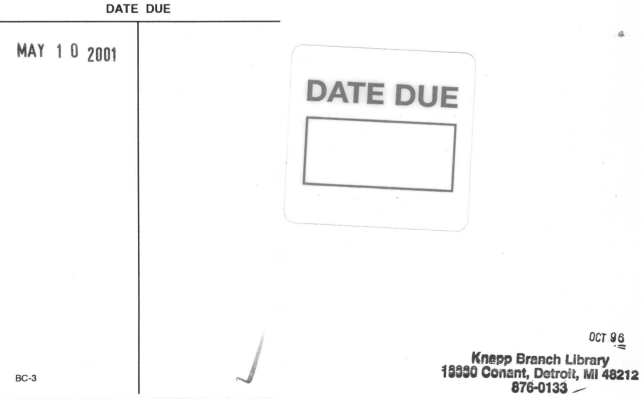

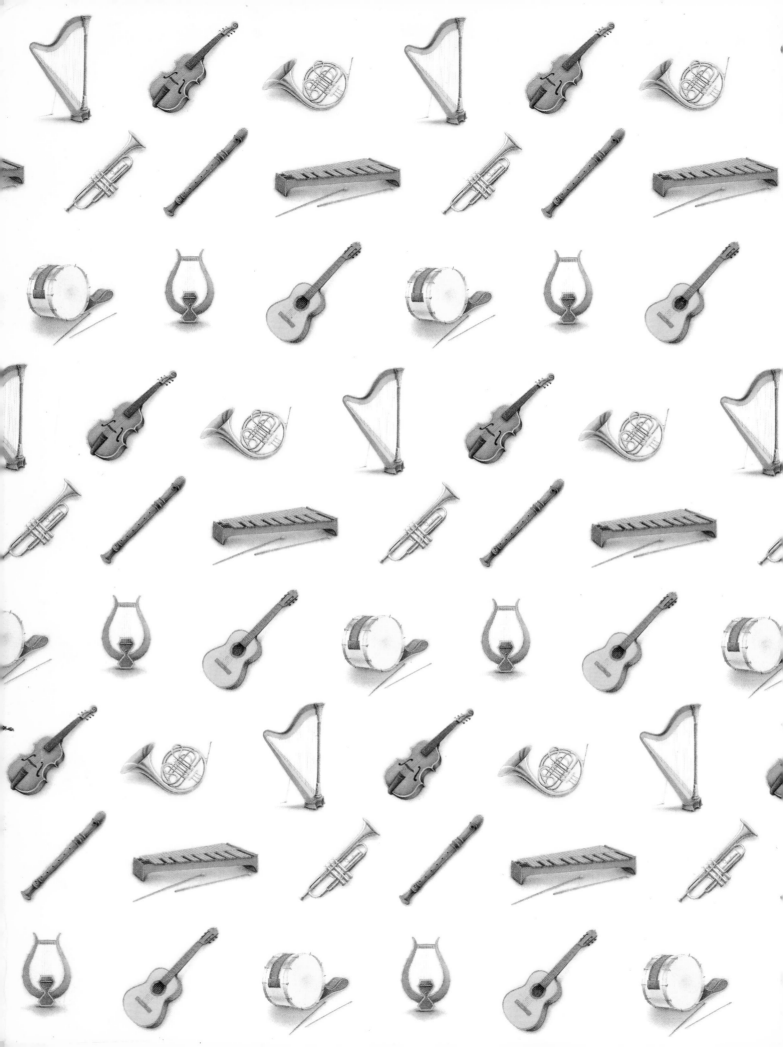

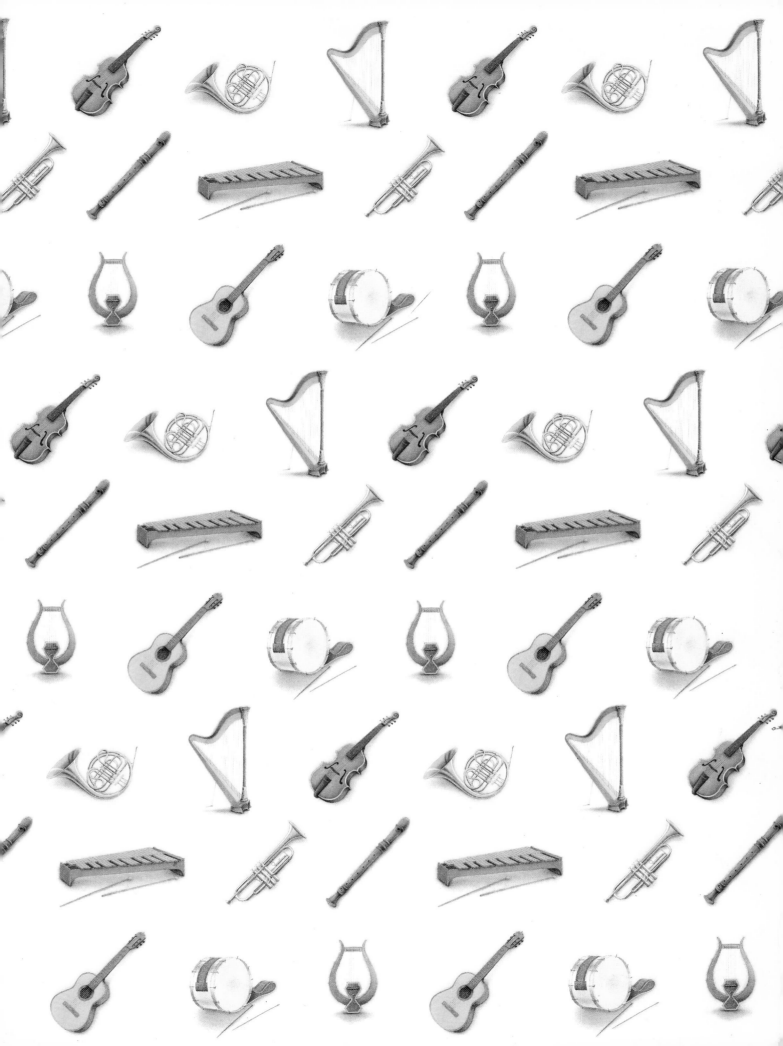

First paperback edition published in the United States,
Great Britain, Canada, Australia, and New Zealand in 1996 by North-South Books,
an imprint of Nord-Süd Verlag AG, Gossau Zürich, Switzerland.

Distributed in the United States by North-South Books Inc., New York.

Library of Congress Cataloging-in-Publication Data
I see the moon: good-night poems and lullabies/selected
and illustrated by Marcus Pfister
Summary: contains traditional lullabies and poems
as well as those of famous poets.
1. Lullabies. 2. Children's Poetry. [1. Poetry—Collections.]
I. Pfister, Marcus, ill.
PN6109.97.I2   1991
808.81'9355—dc20   91-10841

British Library Cataloguing in Publication Data
I see the moon.
I. Pfister, Marcus II. [Weisst du wieviel sternlein stehen]. *English*

ISBN 1-55858-544-3 (PAPERBACK)
1 3 5 7 9 PB 10 8 6 4 2
Printed in Belgium

I See the Moon

Good-Night Poems and Lullabies
Selected and Illustrated by

Marcus Pfister

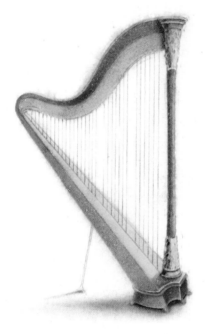

North-South Books

NEW YORK

Night

by William Blake

The sun descending in the west
The evening star does shine;
The birds are silent in their nest,
And I must seek for mine.

The moon like a flower
In heaven's high bower,
With silent delight,
Sits and smiles on the night.

The Sandman Comes

English lullaby

The sandman comes, the sandman comes,
He brings such pretty snow-white sand,
For ev'ry child throughout the land,
The sandman comes.

Lullaby

by Christina Rossetti

Lullaby, oh, lullaby!
Flowers are closed and lambs are sleeping,
Lullaby, oh, lullaby!
Stars are up, the moon is peeping,
Lullaby, oh, lullaby!
While the birds are silence keeping,
Lullaby, oh, lullaby!
Sleep, my baby, fall a-sleeping,
Lullaby, oh, lullaby!

Sleep, My Treasure

by E. Nesbit

Sleep, sleep, my treasure,
The long day's pleasure
Has tired the birds, to their nests they creep;
The garden still is
Alight with lilies,
But all the daisies are fast asleep.

Sleep, sleep, my darling,
Dawn wakes the starling,
The sparrow stirs when he sees day break;
But all the meadow
Is wrapped in shadow,
And you must sleep till the daisies wake!

I See the Moon

Nursery rhyme

I see the moon,
And the moon sees me;
God bless the moon,
And God bless me.

Kumbaya

African-American spiritual

1

Kumbaya my Lord, Kumbaya,
Kumbaya my Lord, Kumbaya,
Kumbaya my Lord, Kumbaya,
Oh Lord, Kumbaya.

2

Someone's crying Lord, Kumbaya,
Someone's crying Lord, Kumbaya,
Someone's crying Lord, Kumbaya,
Oh Lord, Kumbaya.

3

Someone's laughing Lord, Kumbaya,
Someone's laughing Lord, Kumbaya,
Someone's laughing Lord, Kumbaya,
Oh Lord, Kumbaya.

4

Someone's praying Lord, Kumbaya,
Someone's praying Lord, Kumbaya,
Someone's praying Lord, Kumbaya,
Oh Lord, Kumbaya.

5

Someone's sleeping Lord, Kumbaya,
Someone's sleeping Lord, Kumbaya,
Someone's sleeping Lord, Kumbaya,
Oh Lord, Kumbaya.

Golden Slumbers

English lullaby

Golden slumbers kiss your eyes;
Smiles awake you when you rise;
Sleep, pretty baby, do not cry,
And I will sing a lullaby,
Rock then, rock then, lullaby.

The Land of Nod

by Robert Louis Stevenson

From breakfast on through all the day
At home among my friends I stay,
But every night I go abroad
Afar into the land of Nod.

All by myself I have to go,
With none to tell me what to do —
All alone beside the streams
And up the mountain-sides of dreams.

The strangest things are there for me,
Both things to eat and things to see,
And many frightening sights abroad
Till morning in the land of Nod.

Try as I like to find the way,
I never can get back by day,
Nor can I remember plain and clear
The curious music that I hear.

Young Night-Thought

by Robert Louis Stevenson

1

All night long and every night,
When my mama puts out the light,
I see the people marching by,
As plain as day, before my eye.

2

Armies and emperors and kings,
All carrying different kinds of things,
And marching in so grand a way,
You never saw the like by day.

3

So fine a show was never seen
At the great circus on the green;
For every kind of beast and man
Is marching in that caravan.

4

At first they move a little slow,
But still the faster on they go,
And still beside them close I keep
Until we reach the town of Sleep.

Sleep, Baby, Sleep

English lullaby

Sleep, baby, sleep,
Thy father guards the sheep;
Thy mother shakes the dreamland tree
And from it fall sweet dreams for thee,
Sleep, baby, sleep.

Now the Day is Over

by Sabine Baring-Gould

Now the day is over,
    Night is drawing nigh,
Shadows of the evening
    Steal across the sky.

Now the darkness gathers,
    Stars begin to peep,
Birds, and beasts, and flowers
    Soon will be asleep.

Lullaby and Good Night

From the German

Lullaby and good night
With lilies of white
And roses of red
To pillow your head:
May you wake when the day
Chases darkness away,
May you wake when the day
Chases darkness away.

Lullaby and good night
Let angels of light,
Spread wings round your bed
And guard you from dread.
Slumber gently and deep
In the dreamland of sleep,
Slumber gently and deep
In the dreamland of sleep.

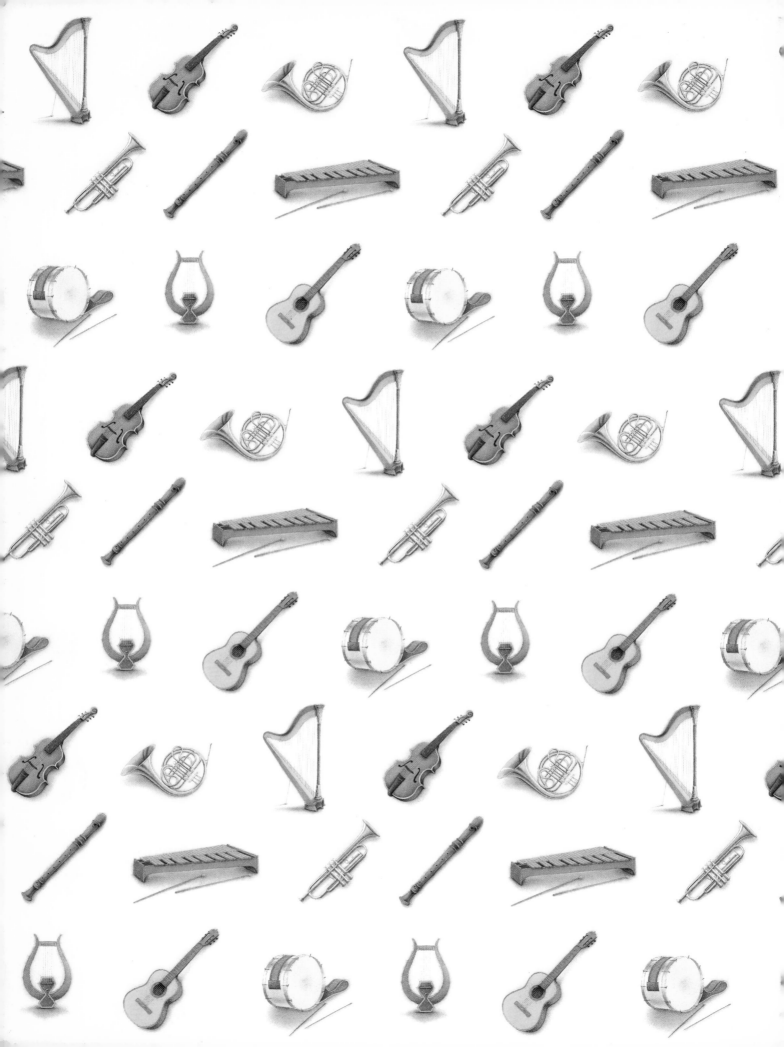